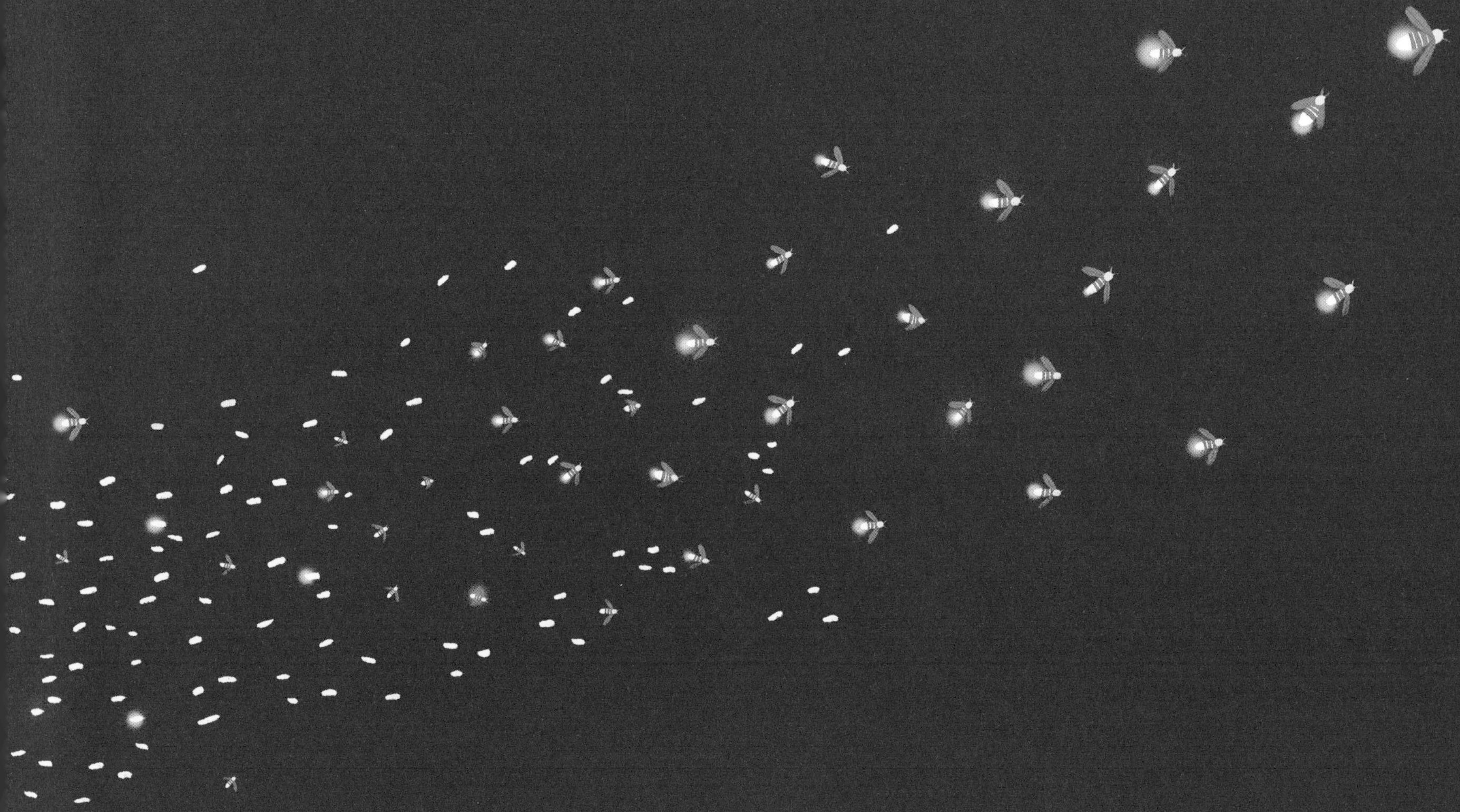

The Usborne Book of
NIGHTTIME

Laura Cowan

Illustrated by Bonnie Pang

Designed by Amy Manning

USBORNE QUICKLINKS

For links to websites where you can watch fireflies flash, see auroras
dance in the sky and discover lots more about nighttime, go to
www.usborne.com/quicklinks and type in the title of this book.
Please follow the internet safety guidelines at the Usborne Quicklinks
website. We recommend that children are supervised while on the internet.

The side of the Earth that faces the Sun is lit up. This is DAY.

The side of the Earth that faces away from the Sun is dark. This is NIGHT, when the only sunlight you can see is bouncing off the Moon.

Zzzzzzzzz

It's bedtime here in India.

Our planet is always turning. That's why it gets dark at night and light in the morning.

We're wide awake!

CONTENTS

Turn the page to explore the world at NIGHT...

G'night, mate!

The Moon looks different on different nights. Sometimes it's big and round, and sometimes it's just a little sliver.

GOODNIGHT?

It's getting DARK. But night isn't ONLY for sleeping – lots of other things are happening, too...

Goodnight, Sun!

Birds are getting ready for bed.

Who's this awake?

MEOW   Cats are just starting to be BUSY.

The police have things to do. They're driving around on patrol.

Twit-twoo!

Foxes and owls wake up for a night of hunting and scavenging.

Mice are awake, too, but they need to WATCH OUT.

It's bedtime for children.

I want to finish this chapter!

I'm staying up late to talk to my friend. She lives on the other side of the world.

Sizzle

Zzzzz

This doctor is working NIGHT SHIFTS at the hospital.

I sleep in the daytime.

One last walk before bed!

WOOF WOOF

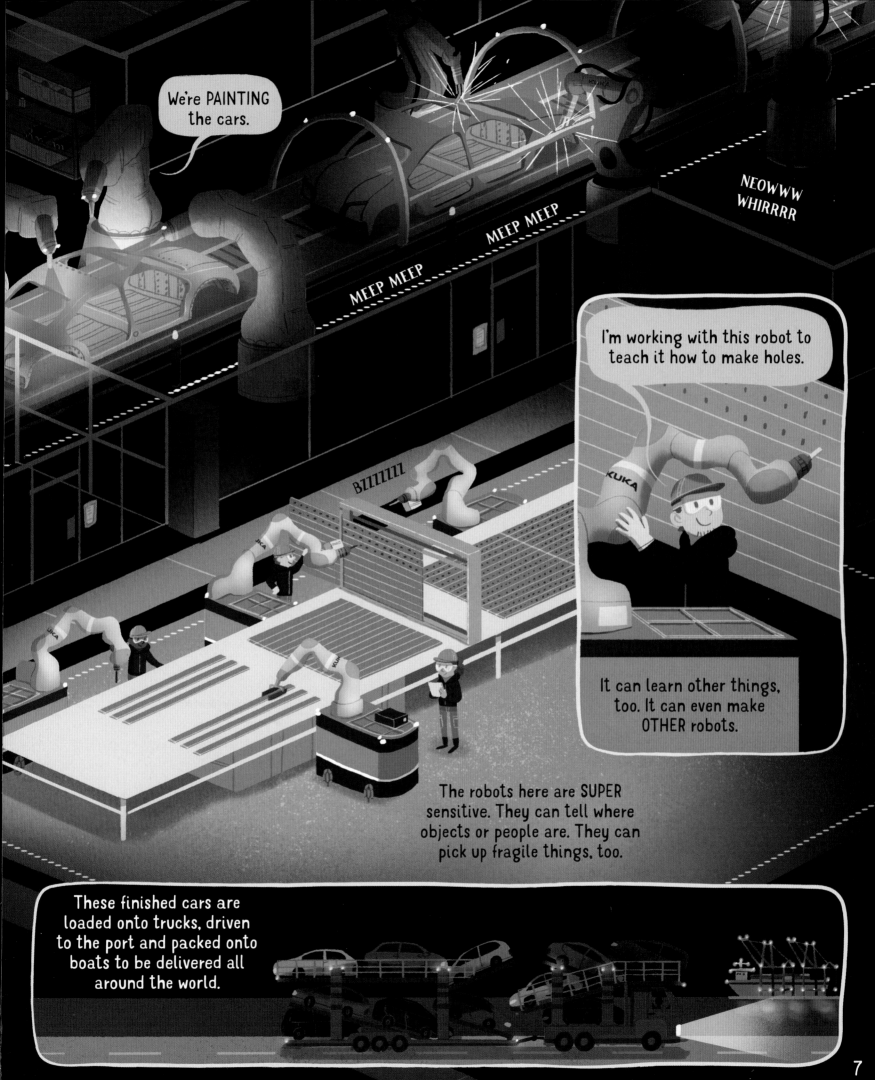

Rabbits are out looking for food. Their babies stay safe underground in the warren where they live.
Sleepy bunnies in bed
But, uh oh, while rabbits are exploring, so are foxes...
RUN, RABBITS, RUN!
Hmmm, what do we have here?
I smell CHICKENS!
And I smell FOX! RUFF RUFF! GET OUT!

BEEP BEEP! TOOT TOOT!

Lots of vehicles keep moving through the night to get people, goods and even pizzas where they need to go.

It's easier for big trucks to get around when the roads are emptier.

BEEP BEEP!

A sleeper train full of sleeping passengers whizzes out of the city...

...past mountains and fields, on its way to new places.

Zzz

Zzzzzzzz

ZZOOOOOOOOOMMMM

I'm going to see my grandchildren. They live far away.

This container train carries all sorts of goods across the country to the port.

PARRRRRRRRRRRRP

When it arrives, the containers are taken off the train and loaded onto a huge ship.

What's in this container ship?

It's carrying lots of new cars. The biggest ships can carry 18,000 cars at once!

NIGHT BENEATH THE WAVES

In shallow waters in warm seas, strange creatures called CORALS come alive at night. And for each type of coral there is one night, once a year – when the temperature's right and the Moon is big – when they make NEW CORALS.

On that night, the corals release eggs into the water.

They're carried along by the waves until they fall to the bottom of the sea and stick to a rock FOREVER.

These rocky shapes that look like plants are all different types of CORALS.

POP

The eggs become NEW corals. They grow their skeletons around themselves, on the OUTSIDE of their bodies.

Lots and LOTS of corals together make a REEF.

POP

MINI fish

On the inside of a coral is its fleshy, squishy, moving body – called a POLYP.

Coral polyps wake up at night and wriggle their tentacles out to feed. And, tonight, to release eggs.

FOREST OF THE NIGHT

Now we're in a dense forest, FULL of creatures.
Can you see their eyes WATCHING you?

Uh oh... CLOUDED LEOPARDS prowl at night.

We can LEAP, too – watch out below!

Clouded leopards can climb STRAIGHT DOWN.

I'm sneaking up on birds, snakes and squirrels to POUNCE on and EAT – mmm mmm MMM.

Wheeeeeeee!

Tarsiers are TINY, but they can jump a long way.

Chirrup!

YUCK! PONGY! That MASSIVE flower STINKS. None of the animals down here will eat it!

Greater mouse deer, oh hello!

The Rafflesia flower smells HORRIBLE and it only blooms at night.

This sun bear is asleep now. But it might wake up and look for food.

Ooh look, here's a Hose's civet. They are VERY RARE and not many people have seen one.

Bearded pig

GRUNT GRUNT GRUNT

SNUFFLE SNUFFLE

Pangolin and BABY pangolin

NIGHT LIGHTS

Night isn't always dark. Not when some creatures light up the night THEMSELVES.

IN THE UNDERGROWTH are...

...GLOW-IN-THE-DARK mushrooms...

FLASH

...and insects, too.

FLASH

IN THE SEA are bright blue sparkles of light – tiny sea creatures called PHYTOPLANKTON.

Woah! Dude!

The phytoplankton make blue light when they are upset by too many waves... or surfers.

IN THE WOODS are hundreds of tiny flecks of LIGHT. They're FIREFLIES.

FLASH

Fireflies are really BEETLES that FLASH to say to other fireflies, HELLO, I'm looking for a FRIEND.

FLASH

Their bottoms are lit up!

But when BABY fireflies flash, it's a message to other creatures, DON'T EAT ME! I'M POISONOUS!

FLASH

FLASH

IN SOUTHEAST ASIA lives a type of snail – Quantula striata – the only land snail in the WHOLE WORLD that can flash.

Our eggs flash!

FLASH

Like fireflies, their flashes are probably a way of talking, a way of saying, HIYA or I'M NOT A SNACK!

And baby snails like me flash, too!

When the snails grow up, some can't flash any more.

19

FAR NORTH

Night near the North Pole is not the same as in other places. In deepest winter, the Sun doesn't reach here for a WHOLE MONTH.

Sometimes a wind from the Sun blows all the way to Earth. It blows dust that smashes into the sky and flashes in all shades of the rainbow. This is the AURORA or NORTHERN LIGHTS.

Reindeer's eyes turn blue in winter without sunlight.

ACK ACK ACK

ARCTIC hares

Shhhhh

GOTCHAAA!

ARCTIC foxes pounce on creatures under the snow.

These animals grow WHITE fur in winter. White fur is good for hiding in the snow, from each other – and from owls!

In the height of summer, for about two months, the Sun NEVER goes down – not even at MIDNIGHT.

Midnight Sun

Reindeer's eyes turn gold in summer when the Sun returns.

Most owls hunt in the dark, but in summer, snowy owls have no choice. They HAVE to hunt in sunlight.

Argh, I don't like sunshine. The hares down there can see me hunting them.

When the snow has melted, Arctic foxes and hares grow brown fur to blend in better with the undergrowth.

You can run, bunnies, but you can't hide!

STARLIGHT, STAR BRIGHT

The night sky is full of light. Especially on a cloudless night when it's sparkling with distant stars...

The Great Dog

Orion

Long ago, people thought the stars made pictures in the sky. They made up stories about them and gave them names.

North Star

Orion was a superhuman warrior in Greek mythology.

Up there is the NORTH STAR. It's bright enough to guide you NORTH in the darkness.

WOOF!

Ooohhhh!

The Moon

You might see JUPITER, a nearby planet. It's like Earth but much bigger and colder.

One of the lights you can see is the International Space Station.

This is the Milky Way galaxy. A galaxy is a group of millions of stars and planets.

ZOOOOM

A shooting star isn't a star at all. It's a ROCK burning up as it falls to Earth from space.

You might see the planet Venus, too.

I can see different things in the sky depending on where I am and what time of year it is.

This telescope is a HUGE eye for seeing faraway things. The Orion Nebula is so far away, even in our fastest space ship, it would take MILLIONS of years to get there.

OUTBACK

It's night in an Australian desert – the OUTBACK. It's very hot, so animals come out in the dark when it's cooler. Some of the ones here don't live ANYWHERE ELSE in the whole world.

NEOWWWWWWWWWW

I'm a doctor. The Outback is HUGE – flying is the quickest way to get to my patients.

So, who's out tonight?

AH-WOOO

AH-WOOO

A big pack of howling DINGOES! AH-WOOO!

Bilbies get all the water they need from eating BUGS.

Thousands of years ago, bilbies lived all over the Outback. But when people came to Australia, so did dingoes, foxes and cats. They hunted down bilbies and now there are only a few left.

Lonnnnng tongue

Tasty treats for me.

SLURP

Flowers close their petals to go to sleep at night. YAWN.

CITIES NEVER SLEEP

Big cities across the world are WIDE AWAKE, too. And after a day of work or study, people go out to enjoy themselves. Anything and everything is happening...

Some artists and writers work while the night goes on outside.

Ideas! I need more ideas!

It feels SPOOKY going to the museum at night!

Museums and art galleries open on some nights for people who are busy in the day.

In cities in HOT countries, people go out dancing at night when it's cooler.

I love to dance the salsa or the tango!

How was your day?

Mmmm, the food here is delicious.

Some cities have parades of fireworks and torches.

It's even dark enough for a LANTERN FESTIVAL.

BOOM DI BOOM

Bang! BANG! Bang! BANNNNNNNG!

AT NIGHT, cities are full of MUSIC.

Opera is VERY LONG, so it doesn't finish until LATE.

TRALALALALALALAAAAAAAA!

Bravo!

ZZZZZzzzzzz

Owwwww, her singing hurts my ears.

At karaoke, people try to entertain EACH OTHER by singing songs.

Jazz music STARTS late, for people who are NIGHT OWLS.

IS THERE NIGHT IN SPACE?

Not exactly, but it's always dark. It looks like night ALL THE TIME on the INTERNATIONAL SPACE STATION.

The station goes all the way around Earth once every 90 minutes. That means the astronauts see 16 sunsets and 16 sunrises EVERY 24 hours (an Earth day). They have to make their own bedtime.

From the station, astronauts can see the WHOLE WORLD.

Yawn! Well, my watch says it's 11 o'clock at night in my hometown.

I'll turn down the temperature and the lights so we can all have a good sleep.

The SUN is coming up.

This light is the line between night and day. It's called THE TERMINATOR.

This is what the AURORA looks like from space.

The Earth is NEVER really dark. Look at all the lights!

The night is lit up by all the streetlights and buildings.

INDEX

INTERNET LINKS

Thank you to KUKA for permission to use images of their robots. KUKA is a leading global supplier of intelligent automation solutions. KUKA offer their customers in the automotive, electronics, consumer goods, metalworking, logistics/e-commerce, healthcare, education and service robotics industries everything they need from a single source: from components and cells to fully automated systems. The KUKA Group is headquartered in Augsburg.

Series editor: Ruth Brocklehurst
Managing designer: Nicola Butler
Digital manipulation: John Russell & Nick Wakeford

Expert advice from John and Margaret Rostron and Dr. Annabel Banks

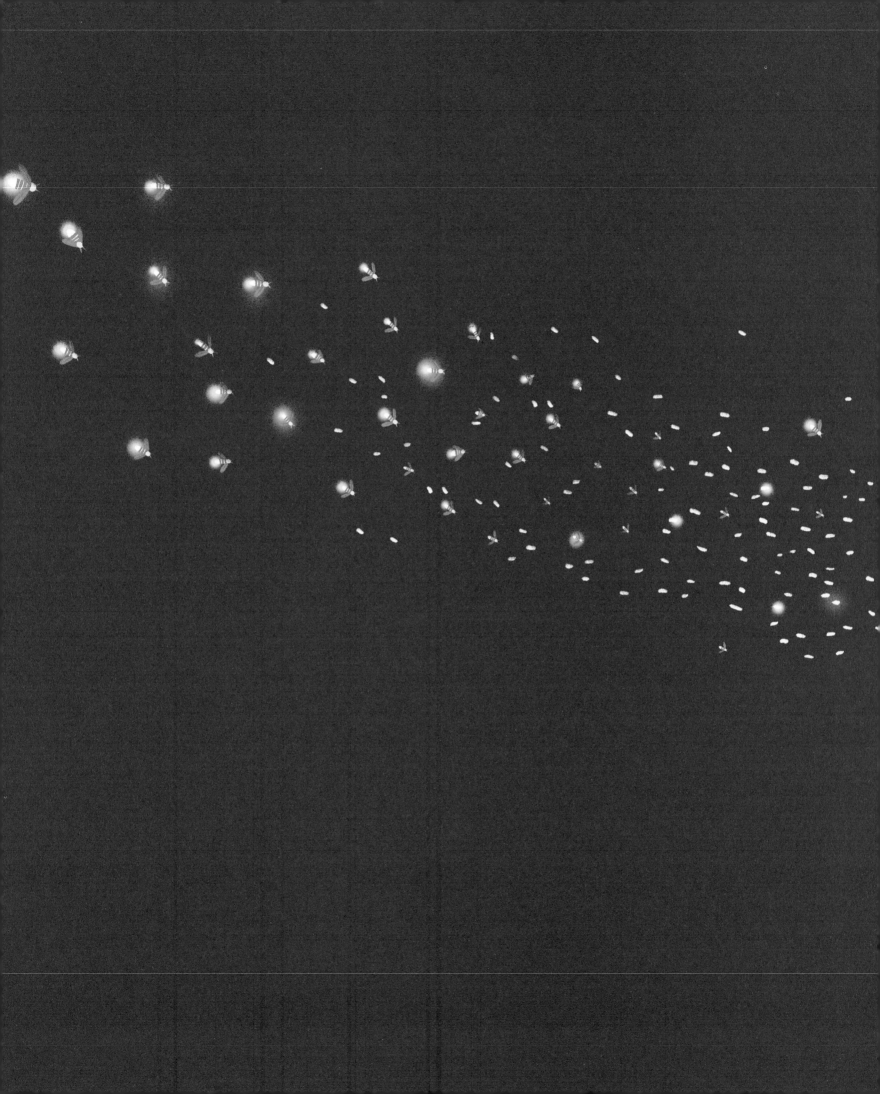